I'M COMING.

I'M SO STUFFED!

I LOVE ROLLING.

I LOVE MUD PUDDLES.

SAM RUNS TO TOWN.

HERE COMES SAM!

SAM ATE THE WHOLE PIE!

SAM WENT INTO BAKERY.

THE BAKER IS SCARED.

THE BAKER JUMPED HIGH.

THE BAKER IS SHAKING.

SAM BUYS AN APPLE PIE.

THANK YOU SAM.

SAM'S CRYING UP THE HILL.

TELL ME WHAT HAPPENED.

SAM WHISPERED.

HERE'S YOUR PRESENT PAPA.

BEST PRESENT I EVER HAD.

SAM ATE AND ATE.

YOUR AMAZING SAM.

NO, I'M SIMPLY SAM.

DOODLING SPACE

www.ingramcontent.com/pod-product-compliance
Lightning Source LLC
Chambersburg PA
CBHW080905120626
46555CB00008B/2970

* 9 7 8 0 6 9 2 5 6 3 7 5 5 *